For Betty Connors and Travis Bogard
with gratitude and admiration
J.G.

For Stella with thanks
A.H.

First published 1995 by Walker Books
87 Vauxhall Walk, London SE11 5HJ

This edition published 1996

10 9 8 7 6 5 4 3 2 1

Text © 1995 Judith Gorog
Illustrations © 1995 Amanda Harvey

This book has been typeset in Columbus MT.

Printed in Hong Kong

British Library Cataloguing in Publication Data
A catalogue record for this book is available from the British Library.

ISBN 0-7445-4776-8

Zilla Sasparilla
-« and the »-
Mud Baby

JUDITH GOROG   *illustrated by* AMANDA HARVEY

WALKER BOOKS
AND SUBSIDIARIES
LONDON • BOSTON • SYDNEY

The way home was a path through the deep woods. That path, all slippery after a solid week of rain, ran alongside Little Muddy River. Zilla put one of her big feet down on a clump of weeds, the other on the driest tuft of grass she could see. She went slowly, trying to keep her shoes out of the sloppy mud.

Once, she peered at the thin, red line where the sun had gone down. Maybe tomorrow would be clear.

"You there. Little Muddy River. Hear me," Zilla insisted. "You don't need more rain, you wicked old river. You don't need to rise up over your banks!"

Lecturing that way, Zilla forgot to watch the path. With a great sucking sound, her left foot disappeared into the muck. Zilla yanked back hard and fell on her bottom. Both feet went into the air, the rest of her very much into the mud.

Zilla stood up, gave her skirt a long sad look, then noticed how cold the ground felt to her naked left foot. Her shoe had disappeared and Zilla wanted it back. She knelt down, took a deep breath, then plunged into the mud with both hands. Right up to her elbows Zilla reached before she felt that shoe. She pulled. The shoe did not budge.

"Oh no you don't," Zilla told the mud. With tremendous effort, she hauled at the shoe, fell backwards with a *thwack*, but cried, "Aha!" all the same.

She sat straight up to look at her muddy hands, thinking that in those hands she would see her left shoe.

Oh my. Sure enough, Zilla's shoe was there, but holding on to the shoe, with both plump fists, was a slithery mud-golden baby, the most beautiful mud baby in the world.

 Zilla wrapped the mud baby in her shawl and cradled him in her arms, singing and coaxing all the while. At last, he let go of her shoe and reached up to touch her face.

Holding that mud baby in her arms, Zilla struggled into her shoe, and started on the long way home. All the while she sang, "Oh my goodness. You wonderful baby. Oh, how I'll care for you."

The mud baby smiled up at her. He gurgled. Surely he agreed.

"And then," Zilla told him, "when I am very old, you'll be a good son and read to me when I can't see." At this the mud baby chortled. Zilla hugged him once more, just to feel that he was real.

Out of the dark woods, away from the river, Zilla walked towards home. Every house had lamps already lit; tables were set for supper. As she approached, doors opened and out came her friends, calling, "Zilla. Zilla. How'd you get so muddy? And is that a genuine mud baby in your arms?"

Zilla told. All her friends sighed in admiration. And every time she finished her telling, someone would ask, "And Zilla, did you get your shoe?"

At last Zilla waved good-bye. For all her singing and telling, she was troubled, so she walked right past her own house and up the hill to a little place set off by itself.

Cinnamon it was. Of course, the news spread. Everyone in the country knew how Zilla Sasparilla had pulled up a mud baby when she'd rescued her shoe. For a week, the path beside the Little Muddy River was crowded with people trying to find a mud baby for themselves. No one did, even though old Mrs Willis plopped her right shoe and her left shoe and her pocketbook deep into the mud and never got a thing back.

Singing, Zilla carried Cinnamon to work in the morning and home again in the evening. She fed him and changed him, bathed him and dried him. She told him rhymes on his fingers and on his toes. She hugged him and kissed him, so glad that he was real.

But worst of all, Cinnamon let go of the mule and dived into the river!

"No!" cried Zilla, but only once. There was Cinnamon, up and down and all around, splashing and laughing, swimming in the river. He helped Zilla clamber up the slippery bank. After that, he swam out to rescue her hat and shawl; though her two big shoes were not to be found.

"Ohhh," warned Zilla, "you mustn't swim alone."

"I didn't." Cinnamon grinned. "You're here."

Zilla sat on the bank – mud from head to toe. Cinnamon and the mule turned the wagon round so they could go back home.

When they got there, Zilla unpacked the wagon and set the house in order. Cinnamon gave the mule food and water, a good rub-down and a name.

Before the weather got cold, Cinnamon and the mule earned enough money to buy Zilla a new pair of shoes.

And, if she has not lost them, Zilla is wearing them still.